Praise for *Good Dog McTavish*

"A hilarious story about a special rescue dog who makes a difference in surprising ways" *Scotsman*

"Warm family drama full of wry humour and a really excellent dog" *Bookseller*

"A clever, funny and extremely stylish novella, and a wonderful bit of domestic satire" Lovereading4kids, Andrea Reece

"Full of Meg's wry humour and beautiful prose, this is a story for the young and young at heart" Books Are My Bag

"Common sense has rarely been so charmingly conveyed" *New Statesman*

"This brilliantly charming and heart-warming short novel is full of spark, keen observations and sly humour" Book Trust

"A laugh-aloud, entertaining story with larger-than-life characters, especially the captivating dog. I can't wait to hear more about him" *Primary Times*

"What a lovely short story. Recommended to boys and girls, especially those who like dogs" Lovereading4kids reviewer Tomasz, age 11

McTavish

GOES

WILD

McTAVISH
GOES
WILD

Meg Rosoff

With illustrations by Grace Easton

Conkers

Conkers

First published in 2018 in Great Britain by
Barrington Stoke Ltd
18 Walker Street, Edinburgh, EH3 7LP

www.barringtonstoke.co.uk

Text © 2018 Meg Rosoff
Illustrations © 2018 Grace Easton

A CIP catalogue record for this book is available
from the British Library upon request

ISBN: 978-1-78112-761-2

Printed in Great Britain by Clays Ltd, St Ives plc

CONTENTS

1

School's Out!

Betty Peachey opened her eyes.

She could hear birds singing. She could see sun shining. The air felt warm. Outside her window, bees buzzed and flowers nodded in the breeze.

She listened carefully. There was no shouting and no rushing about. No one was pounding on the bathroom door or stamping

down the stairs. There was no smell of burning

toast from the kitchen.

In the next room, her brother was still

asleep.

In the room next to that, her sister was

reading the works of a German philosopher

whose name no one could spell.

Downstairs, Betty's parents ate breakfast

and read the newspaper.

The house was quiet except for the sound

of turning pages and munching.

Summer! Betty thought. *The first day of*

the summer holidays is the happiest day of the year. *Even happier than Christmas.*

Lying in her bed, with the sun streaming in through the window, Betty sighed. *I must be the happiest girl in the world*, she thought.

Lying on his bed under the stairs, McTavish sighed. *I must be the happiest dog in the world*, McTavish thought. For there is nothing a dog likes more than to have his entire pack all gathered together peacefully in one place.

McTavish had made a great deal of progress with the Peachey family since deciding to rescue them, but they still required hard work and patience.

Pa Peachey could be extremely stubborn. Ollie Peachey could be argumentative. Ava Peachey tended to read too much German philosophy and come up with too many theories.

Only Betty Peachey and her mother were the sort of calm, sensible, well-behaved humans that dogs prefer to share a home with.

Training the Peachey family had been slow and difficult, but he was an intelligent dog and was up to the job. He understood that a family with an uncertain and chaotic past could

not be fixed overnight. With a combination

of love, patience and consistent handling, he

had helped the Peacheys become far more

organised and relaxed than when he had first

decided to rescue them.

But there was still a long way to go.

2

The Peacheys Choose a Holiday

"Well," said Pa Peachey, when everyone had finally come down to breakfast. "Summer is upon us, and it is time we chose a destination for our family holiday."

"I would like to go to a place with loud discos every night so I can meet many beautiful girls who will want to be my girlfriend," said Ollie.

"I would like to visit the birthplace of the philosopher Friedrich Nietzsche in Germany," said Ava. "There, I will think about philosophy night and day."

"A yoga retreat in India would be perfect," mused Ma Peachey. "There, I might finally achieve my dream of striking a one-handed tree pose."

Betty Peachey was silent.

Everybody looked at her.

At last she took a deep breath.

"I," she said, "would like to go camping."

"CAMPING?" The Peacheys were aghast.

"Camping? With horrible creeping crawling biting bugs?" said Ava.

"Camping? In the freezing rain? On the cold hard ground?" said Ollie. "With no wi-fi and nowhere to charge your phone?"

"Camping? With poisonous snakes and rats and killer moles?" said Pa Peachey.

There was a long silence during which the Peacheys gaped at Betty.

"Yes," said Betty. "Camping."

McTavish crept out of his bed under the stairs to listen.

"For one thing," Betty said, "camping is

educational. You pitch your own tent and cook

your own food. Camping builds camaraderie

and cooperation. It requires skills, like making

fires and reading maps. You learn new things

and live side by side with nature."

"I don't want to live side by side with

nature," said Ollie. "I want a girlfriend."

"I don't want camaraderie," said Ava,

glaring at Ollie. "Especially if it's with him."

"Nature?" said Pa Peachey. "Nature is full

of bears and Tasmanian devils. Nature is just

another word for swamps and getting struck by

lightning. Nature is falling out of a canoe and

drowning. Or getting malaria from mosquitoes.

Nature is having to eat crickets or starve to

death. I hate nature."

Everyone looked at Pa Peachey.

"Nature," said Betty, "is the wind blowing

gently through the trees. It is the sun warming

your face. It is the smell of damp earth and

the sound of blackbirds singing. Nature is

green shoots and new buds. It is daffodils and

buttercups. I love nature."

For a long moment, none of the Peacheys

said a word.

At last, Ma Peachey spoke. "I think camping

is an excellent idea. For one thing, it is not
expensive. For another, it does not require
mobile phones or laptops. And for a third thing,
if we went camping, we would not have to put
McTavish in a kennel. We could take him with us."

Everyone looked at McTavish, who wagged
his tail. In his opinion, this was the best
argument in favour of camping.

He walked over to Betty and lay at her
feet. Well, not actually at her feet but on her
feet.

Pa Peachey shook his head. "This flirtation
with nature is a travesty," he said. "It will all

end in tears." But nobody paid much attention,

because that is what Pa Peachey always said,

about practically everything.

3

Going Camping

Betty and Ma Peachey borrowed a tent from Ma Peachey's brother, who was a great camping enthusiast and loved the outdoors. "You will have the most wonderful time camping," he said. "You will become closer to nature and closer to each other. You will feel healthier and happier. There is nothing so healthy and happy as camping."

As they carried the tent home in the car, Betty and Ma Peachey discussed where they should go on their holiday.

"Perhaps we should go to the beach," Betty said.

"Or to the mountains," Ma Peachey said.

As they entered the house, Ollie emerged from his bedroom. "I have been checking the internet," he called down. "I have found a campsite with its own disco."

"I think I'll just stay home," said Ava. "And begin my study of Immanuel Kant. I know lamentably little about metaphysics." No one understood what Ava was talking about, as usual.

Pa Peachey came in from mowing the lawn. "I hope you have abandoned this absurd notion about 'camping'."

Ma Peachey and Betty put the tent down on the floor. "We have a tent," said Betty. "All we need now is a place to pitch it."

"Well," said Pa Peachey. "There are infinite possibilities. We could pitch it in a field full of angry bulls. We could pitch it on a hornets' nest. We could pitch it next to a river filled with man-eating pirhanas. The world is crammed with likely places to pitch a tent."

Ma Peachey had a thoughtful look on her face. "I have an idea," she said, and disappeared up to her office.

Everyone waited.

Ma Peachey returned with a map.

"This is it!" said Ma Peachey, opening the map on the kitchen table.

All the Peacheys leaned in to look.

"Before Pa Peachey and I were married, I went camping on a faraway farm in a beautiful meadow next to a sparkling river beside a majestic mountain. We had the most wonderful time." Ma Peachey's face looked dreamy all of a sudden.

Pa Peachey's eyes narrowed. "We? Who was we?"

"That is not correct grammar," Ma Peachey said, snapping back to reality. "It was right ..." she searched, and then pointed with her finger, "here."

"'Faraway Campsite,'" read Ollie.

Pa Peachey frowned. "But ..."

"It looks perfect!" said Betty.

"Is there a disco?" asked Ollie.

"There is no disco," Ma Peachey said, "but we can camp in the meadow and climb the mountain and swim in the river. And dogs are very welcome when accompanied by humans."

Betty kneeled down and hugged McTavish. "If dogs are welcome, then it must be a good place."

McTavish was glad to be accompanying the Peacheys on holiday. But he was also wondering what it would be like to have five wild Peacheys running this way and that in a meadow at the edge of a river beside a mountain.

It might be fun, he thought.

Or it might be chaos.

He would have to wait and see.

4

The Peacheys Set Off

"Sleeping bags?"

"Check."

"Socks?"

"Check."

"Frying pan?"

"Check."

"Map?"

"Check."

"Chocolate?"

"Check."

"Toothpaste?"

Betty looked surprised. "I didn't know we needed to take toothpaste. I thought we'd make our own toothpaste out of ..." She paused. "Out of bark and sand."

"Bark and sand would make very unpleasant toothpaste," Ma Peachey said. "I think it might be easier just to bring our own."

Betty added toothpaste to her rucksack.

"Well," said Ma Peachey, "I think we're set. Is everybody set?"

"Yes," said Ava. "I have two volumes of Immanuel Kant, one of Jean-Paul Sartre, a slim volume of Descartes and a book called *The Problem of Philosophy*."

"The problem of philosophy," Ollie said, "is that it is far too boring."

"No it's not," said Ava.

"Yes it is," said Ollie.

"No it's not."

"Yes it is."

"No it's n—"

"That's quite enough," said Ma Peachey. "If Ava wants to take books, she may take books.

Ollie, are you packed?"

"I am packed," Ollie said. "I have my best shirt, deodorant, cologne, hairdryer, styling gel—"

"Ollie thinks he will meet a beautiful farmer's daughter," Ava crowed. "And that she will want to be his girlfriend."

"I do not," Ollie said.

"You do too," Ava said.

"I do not," Ollie said.

"You do too," Ava said.

"Enough!" Ma Peachey said. "Pa Peachey? What have you packed?"

Pa Peachey dragged a very heavy suitcase into the room. "I have mosquito repellent for tsetse flies and shark repellent for sharks. I have bottles of aspirin and splints for broken bones. I have bandages and plasters, flares for emergency rescue. I have water purification tablets and whistles. I have face masks in case of hazardous waste, a loudhailer, foil blankets and sterile dressings. I have enough freeze-dried meals for a month in case we are snowed in."

Ma Peachey closed her eyes.

"I also have a foldable ladder, pepper spray

for defence against bears, and five thermal survival bags that will keep us warm at temperatures down to minus fifty," Pa Peachey continued.

"It is summer," Ma Peachey said, opening her eyes at last. "I feel certain that temperatures will not sink to minus fifty. Betty?"

"I have the food, the map, the tent, the tarp, the sleeping bags and the directions," Betty replied.

"Thank you, Betty. It's nice to know there is at least one other member of the family who is not completely insane," said Ma Peachey.

"Also," Betty said, "I have a bed, bowl and lead for McTavish."

"And a dog tent," Pa Peachey said.

All the Peacheys looked at him.

"McTavish does not need a dog tent," Betty said. "He will sleep in our tent."

"A dog in our tent? *In our tent?* Now that is the last straw. I suppose on this camping trip you will also expect us to sleep on the ground, eat from bowls and pee against trees like dogs?" Pa Peachey shook his head sadly. "That it should come to this."

Everyone pretended he had not spoken.

"OK," Ma Peachey said, "if everyone is ready, let's go."

5

Faraway Campsite

They drove and they drove. And they drove and they drove some more.

The drive was not peaceful.

Ava wanted to talk about philosophy, but nobody wanted to listen.

Ollie was hungry.

Betty needed to go to the toilet.

Ollie punched Betty when she fell asleep on him.

Betty complained to Ma Peachey.

Ma Peachey complained about Pa Peachey's driving. Pa Peachey complained about Ma Peachey's driving.

McTavish sighed. *What a badly behaved family*, he thought. He sat on Betty's lap and looked out the window.

Sometimes Betty opened the window so McTavish could stick out his head and let his ears blow in the wind. All dogs like to feel their ears blowing in the wind, though nobody knows why.

After a while, they turned off the motorway onto an A road.

After another while, they turned off the A road onto a B road.

After another while, they turned off the B road onto a very narrow road with a line of grass down the middle.

At the end of the very narrow road, a sign read "Faraway Campsite ½ mile".

"We're almost there," said Ma Peachey, turning onto an even narrower road. (It wasn't even a real road – it was a dirt track.)

At the end of the dirt track, Ma Peachey

stopped the car. A small sign read "Park Here".

No other cars were parked there.

They parked. In front of them was a

beautiful meadow full of wild flowers. To one

side was a cool rushing river, not so big that

you couldn't cross it and not so small that

you couldn't swim in it. To the other side was

a dark-green mountain rising up behind the

river. The mountain was small enough to climb.

"Oh," said Betty in a soft voice. "I have

never seen a place so beautiful."

Ma Peachey sighed. "It is just as I remember

it from last time, before I met your father."

Pa Peachey frowned. "Who did you say you came here with?"

Ma Peachey smiled a faraway smile.

Ollie looked around. "Well," he said, "considering there is no disco, this is not so bad."

Ava was staring into space. "I think Jean-Paul Sartre would like it here," she said. "It is very existential." As usual, nobody had any idea what she was talking about.

McTavish stood for a moment looking out at the meadow. It was the most dog-friendly meadow he had ever seen. It had no fence. It had no sign reading "Keep off the grass" or "All dogs must be kept on a lead". It had no cars rushing past. It had no broken glass or chunks of concrete. McTavish stood for one moment just sniffing. And then he began to run.

He ran from one end of the meadow to the other. He ran around in happy circles. He leaped and he jumped for joy. Then he ran down to the river, put his front paws in the water and had a drink. The water in the river tasted delicious. It tasted so delicious that he decided to wade in, deeper and deeper, until his feet left the ground and he found he was swimming.

"McTavish can swim!" shouted Betty. "Good

dog, McTavish!"

McTavish swam and swam while the

Peacheys unpacked the car. They unpacked

the tent and the sleeping bags and Ava's

philosophy books and Pa Peachey's emergency

supplies. They unpacked Ollie's hairdryer, even

though there was no place to plug it in. They

finished unpacking just as McTavish finished

swimming.

McTavish ran out of the river, bounded up

to the family and shook the water out of his

coat.

"Bad dog, McTavish!" shouted everyone at once.

McTavish looked much smaller and skinnier with a wet coat. But he still looked wise and sensible. He also looked very happy.

Meanwhile, Pa Peachey began to put up the tent. It was a large tent with three rooms. It had many pegs and many poles and many ropes. Pa Peachey had no idea how to put up a tent. He tried for some time to figure out which rope went with which peg, but in the end he claimed the tent was broken and walked away.

Ma Peachey took over. She knew how to

put up a tent. She attached the proper ropes to the proper pegs. She spread the tarp and connected the poles. She hooked the poles through the proper loops and pushed the ends through the proper holes. With a bit of help from Ollie and Ava and Betty, Ma Peachey had the tent up in no time at all.

It was a lovely tent. You could stand up in all three rooms. Ma and Pa Peachey took possession of the largest room. The smallest room went to Ollie. And the middle-sized room went to Ava, Betty and McTavish.

Each room had a window made of mesh.

Betty blew up her air mattress and spread her sleeping bag on top of it, under the window. At the foot of her bed, she arranged McTavish's bed. He came and lay down just to test it. Betty and McTavish agreed that their beds were very comfortable indeed.

Ava was already lying on her bed reading Jean-Paul Sartre. Ollie was dozing in his tiny room. Ma Peachey was changing out of her clothes and into her swimsuit.

"Come for a swim!" she called as she headed down to the river.

McTavish followed close behind. For

although most dogs are natural swimmers, he had no idea whether any of the Peacheys could do more than flounder about in a helpless and hazardous manner.

McTavish took his job as rescue dog very seriously, and he wondered if the Peacheys might have to be rescued.

Betty changed into her swimsuit and ran after Ma Peachey. Pa Peachey hurried down to the river carrying a life jacket and a can of shark repellent.

"There are five true species of river shark," Pa Peachey explained. "They may be rare, but even a rare shark can bite off your arm."

"This river does not have sharks," said Ma Peachey to her husband.

McTavish sympathised with Pa Peachey just the tiniest bit. Most rivers did not have sharks – this much was true. But they did have dangerous currents, entangling weeds and hidden depths. McTavish knew such dangers were uncommon, but he felt he should keep watch on the Peacheys, just in case they did something silly.

Which was, he thought, *extremely likely.*

6

"Do Your Ears Hang Low?"

Despite noises in the night, most of which were made by Ollie pretending to be a grizzly bear, all the Peacheys slept very well in the tent.

The next morning, Betty volunteered to make breakfast.

Pa Peachey made coffee.

Ava made a fire.

Ollie slept.

Ma Peachey produced a frying pan, some sausages, a loaf of bread and some eggs.

Betty cooked the sausages over the fire. Then she fried the eggs. While everything else was cooking, Ava and Pa Peachey toasted slices of bread on a long fork over the fire, which worked almost as well as a toaster. Nobody minded that the bread was a little bit burned.

They all ate sausage and egg sandwiches, including McTavish, whose favourite food was pretty much anything. Ollie managed to get out of bed exactly when breakfast was ready.

Afterwards, everyone was happy. They

had a good tent, a good breakfast, the sun was

shining and, so far at least, there was no sign

of bears, wolverines, sharks or killer bees.

"What shall we do now?" asked Ava, as

Ollie skulked back in the direction of his

sleeping bag.

"We could go for a hike," suggested Ma

Peachey.

But Ava did not want to go for a hike.

Reading Jean-Paul Sartre was exhausting

enough, she said. Ollie did not want to go on a

hike either, as he said it would interfere with

his sleep. Pa Peachey did not want to go on a

hike in case of ambush by mountain lions.

McTavish and Betty thought a walk was an excellent idea.

"Take this!" insisted Pa Peachey, handing his wife a large and very heavy rucksack.

"What's in it?" asked Ma Peachey.

"Only the bare essentials," said Pa Peachey. "Flares, a club to beat away mountain lions, snakebite anti-venom, emergency blankets, rations for a week, two inflatable life jackets, one compass, one knife, one signal mirror and a book entitled *Teach Yourself Morse Code*."

"*Teach Yourself Morse Code?* Will we have time to teach ourselves Morse Code in an emergency?" Ma Peachey asked.

"It depends on the emergency," answered Pa Peachey. "If it is a very long drawn-out emergency, such as being kept hostage in a cave by bears for many months, there will be time to learn Morse Code – and probably French as well."

Ma Peachey thought about this for a moment. "I think," she said, "that we will leave the emergency supplies here, as we are planning quite a simple walk. If anything goes wrong, and it looks as if we are likely to be held hostage by bears for many months, we will send McTavish back to notify you. He is, after all, a rescue dog."

"McTavish is a *rescued* dog. It is not at all the same as a *rescue* dog," said Pa Peachey. "A *rescued* dog requires someone to rescue him. A *rescue* dog is a highly trained professional animal capable of reacting instantly in an emergency to save lives or sniff out people buried in an earthquake."

Betty considered McTavish. McTavish considered Betty. "I believe McTavish is both *rescued* and entirely capable of rescui*ng*," Betty said. "In fact, I feel quite certain that McTavish would be a first-rate companion in any emergency. I always feel safe when McTavish is by my side."

McTavish shot Pa Peachey a smug look.

"Ho ho," said Pa Peachey. "Perhaps you're right. Perhaps if the emergency involved sausages nobody wanted to eat, then McTavish would take care of them. Perhaps if the emergency involved needing a dog to lie on his bed and doze, then McTavish would be a hero."

Betty looked at her father. "Never

underestimate McTavish. He is the smartest, most loyal, intelligent dog I have ever met."

"Enough!" Ma Peachey said. "We will take a map and leave our emergency supplies behind, just this once." And off she went with McTavish and Betty.

For some time, McTavish, Betty and Ma Peachey walked along the river. McTavish chased rabbits and butterflies. Betty and Ma Peachey talked about this and that. They stopped every once in a while to admire the beautiful river and the sunny meadow. When they felt hot, they went in for a swim.

Eventually, when they had walked long enough in one direction, they turned around and walked back along the river to the campsite.

"Thank goodness you made it home alive," said Pa Peachey, who ran trembling to greet them. "You've been gone for nearly three hours. I was about to call out the air rescue."

"We had a very pleasant walk, thank you, dear," Ma Peachey replied. "A very pleasant and uneventful walk indeed."

Betty had collected a bunch of wild flowers, some of which she now plaited together to make a crown for McTavish.

McTavish looked very handsome in his crown.

That night, they cooked two fish that Ava had caught in the river and ate them with potatoes roasted in foil. Then they toasted marshmallows on sticks over the embers.

Everything tasted delicious.

"Now, shall we sing songs around the campfire?" asked Betty.

"That's the silliest idea I ever heard," said Ollie.

"I don't know any campfire songs," said Ava.

"Loud noises such as singing are likely to attract bears," said Pa Peachey.

Betty looked sad. But just then McTavish threw back his head and began to sing the song of the ancient campfire wolf.

"Aaaaaoooooooowww!" sang McTavish. "AAAAAAOOOOOOOWOOWOOOO!!!!"

Ollie and Ava put their hands over their ears. Ma and Pa Peachey did the same. Even Betty found the noise a bit loud.

In order to drown it out, Betty began to sing. She sang the first thing that came into her head, which was "Do Your Ears Hang Low?"

Soon, the entire Peachey family was singing "Do Your Ears Hang Low?" as loudly as they could. By verse three, they hit their stride and were making nearly as much noise as McTavish. By verse four, McTavish had stopped howling. By verse six (which only Betty knew), McTavish was entirely silent.

The Peacheys were on a roll. After singing "Do Your Ears Hang Low?", they sang a number of other songs, such as "O Little Town Of Bethlehem" (even though it wasn't Christmas), "Row Row Row The Boat", "Great Tom Is Cast", "Glory Glory How Peculiar" and other campfire favourites. Until everyone was tired and ready for bed.

McTavish followed them into the tent and waited until everyone else had dropped off to sleep before he put his head on his paws and shut his eyes. Within minutes, he too was fast asleep.

7

Damp Camp

On day two of camping it rained. And it rained
and it rained and it rained.

Nobody wanted to leave the tent, which
was somewhat drier than the outdoors.

Nobody wanted to try to make a fire in
the rain.

Breakfast was cold bread and butter.

Lunch was peanut butter and pickle sandwiches.

By suppertime, every single Peachey was damp and cross and hungry.

The nearest town was six miles away. It was nice to be able to pitch a tent six miles from civilisation. But now that the Peacheys needed a restaurant, it was inconvenient. Everyone was bickering and fed up with being damp, so they all piled into the car and drove six miles to the nearest town.

In the nearest town, there was a small restaurant with a large sign on the door. The sign read "No Dogs Allowed".

"But what about McTavish?" asked Betty. "He is just as hungry and damp as the rest of us!"

"He will have to have his supper in the car," said Ma Peachey. "There is nothing else to be done."

The five Peacheys, minus McTavish, trooped into the restaurant and ordered delicious hot meals. Betty also ordered two large burgers, no buns, cooked very rare for McTavish. When they arrived, she took them out to the car.

"I am very sorry, dear McTavish. The

restaurant does not allow dogs, so you shall have to eat your dinner in the car." But McTavish was too busy eating his burgers to worry about the restaurant's pet policy.

After the Peacheys had eaten, they all piled into the car and drove back to their miserable damp tent.

"I want to go home," said Ava.

"So do I," said Ollie.

"I'm afraid I agree. Camping is far too dangerous," said Pa Peachey. "With all this rain, I feel certain the river will overflow its banks and we shall be drowned in our sleep."

"Nonsense," said Ma Peachey. "The weather report for tomorrow is for sunshine."

On that note, they all went to sleep, damp and bad-tempered and dreaming of their lovely dry home.

But the following morning the sun was shining, the earth was dry, the birds were singing and the sky was blue. It was a beautiful day.

"Let's go home," said Ollie.

"If we leave now, we'll make it in time for lunch," said Ava.

"Of course, we need to drive slowly and

carefully to avoid fatal accidents," said Pa

Peachey. "If we were to hit a moose on the

motorway, we'd all be killed."

"A moose?" asked Betty.

Nobody bothered to reply.

"I think today is the perfect day for our

all-day hike with a picnic lunch," Ma Peachey

said. "I've made the picnic and packed it in my

rucksack. All we have to do is set off."

"Nope," said Ollie.

"No way," said Ava.

"Bad idea," said Pa Peachey, shaking his

head. "Rattlesnakes."

"Rattlesnakes?" asked Ma Peachey.

"Where's McTavish?" asked Betty.

"He's right here – well, he was right here a minute ago," Ollie said.

"McTavish!" called Ma Peachey. "McTavish, where are you?"

There was no answer.

"He's probably been eaten by mountain lions," said Pa Peachey. "When they get hungry, they creep down out of the mountains looking for prey. They stalk silently and kill with a single blow ..."

"McTavish!" called Betty. "Where are you, McTavish?"

All was silent. They listened very hard, hoping to hear the noise of panting in the meadow, a rustling in a hedge, a splashing in the river or the faraway bark of McTavish chasing a rabbit.

Nothing.

"McTAVISH!" called Pa Peachey. "McTAVISH, COME OUT FROM WHERE YOU ARE HIDING AT ONCE!"

But there was no answer. And no McTavish.

With a stricken look, Betty began running in the direction of the river. "He must have gone this way!" she shouted.

Everyone ran after her. Pa Peachey and
Ava shouted "Betty!" while Ollie and Ma Peachey
shouted "McTavish!" The combined noise of
five Peacheys shouting different names caused
birds to lift off from trees and fish to dive deep
down to the bottom of the river. If there had
been any mountain lions within fifty miles,
they would have been cowering in their dens.

"McTavish!" shouted Betty.

"McTAVISH!" shouted Ma Peachey.

"BETTY!" shouted Ava.

"SLOW DOWN!" shouted Pa Peachey, who
was panting.

The shouting Peachey clan came to a bridge over the river. Without hesitation, they crossed, shouting "McTavish!" and "Here, boy!" and "Where are you, you silly dog?" and occasionally "This is hopeless."

Just then, Ava stopped. "What's that over there?" she asked, pointing.

All the Peacheys looked in the direction that Ava pointed. About half a mile away, there appeared to be something McTavish-shaped and McTavish-coloured loping steadily towards the mountain.

"McTavish?" Ollie squinted at the

McTavish-shaped object.

"McTavish?" asked Pa Peachey.

"McTavish," Betty sighed. She set off once more at a run.

The family followed.

8

McTavish Leads the Peacheys Astray

McTavish stopped for a drink at a lovely

sky-blue mountain lake. He waded in up to his

chin and waited for the delicious cool water

to soak through his coat. Standing in the lake

made him feel cool all over. There were certain

disadvantages of having a warm coat on a

warm summer's day.

Particularly if one was moving at a brisk pace.

McTavish had been moving at a brisk pace. *It's the only way*, he thought. The Peachey family needed rescuing from bickering and laziness. And being a rescue dog, McTavish felt that it was his job to rescue them.

It is worth noting that the average speed of a running dog is approximately nineteen miles per hour. The average speed of a running human is about half that. So if a dog wanted to lead a group of humans on a very long wild-goose chase up into a mountain, it would prove about half as taxing for the dog as for the people.

McTavish tried to keep this in mind as he set off. He considered himself something of an unofficial Peachey tour guide, for it had become clear to him that they would never explore the beautiful mountain if he didn't take action.

In the meantime, it was very pleasant just floating around in the lake like a crocodile, his eyes above water, his tail slowly wafting from side to side as he paddled about.

Meanwhile, the mountain echoed with cries of "McTavish!" and "Come back!"

As the cries came closer to the beautiful lake, McTavish paddled slowly over to the far side, stepped out of the water, shook himself dry and scampered a short distance away, where he climbed up on a large boulder with a clear view of everything below. There, he waited.

After about ten minutes, he saw the Peachey family arrive at the lake. They looked tired and dusty and very fed up, and for a moment McTavish felt a small pang of guilt.

Poor Peacheys, he thought, but then corrected himself sternly. *They are not at all poor. They are merely lazy and argumentative.*

Except for Betty and Ma Peachey, that is.

McTavish lay on the large boulder and watched his family. At first, they were too cross to notice how beautiful the mountain lake was. They were too tired to notice the lovely flowers around the edge or the birds flitting along the surface. They paid no attention to the sparkling reflections the sun cast on the water.

But then Ava squatted down and made a cup of her hands to drink from the cool clear lake.

Ollie waded in up to his waist and, when

he thought no one was looking, slid happily

under the water and began to swim, emerging

spouting and spluttering like a seal.

Just at that moment, McTavish made a

small, distinct "woof".

"Look!" cried Betty. "It's McTavish! He isn't

lost. He's just resting on that rock."

"Bad dog, McTavish," Pa Peachey said.

"Come here this instant!"

But McTavish did not move.

"As long as we are here, I think we should

swim in the beautiful lake," said Ma Peachey.

"McTavish will come back to us when he is ready."

She had already begun to wonder whether
McTavish had his own reasons for luring them up
the mountain. Now she felt quite sure of it.

Pa Peachey stood with his arms crossed at
the edge of the lake. "You are all very foolish,"
he said. "There may be poisonous sea urchins
and brain-eating parasites in this lake."

"There may be," replied Ma Peachey, "and
then again, there may not." She waded into
the lake, and as the cool water swirled round
her dusty legs, she gave a little cry of glee and
dunked under, splashing Ollie as she went.

Soon, all the Peacheys (with the exception

of Pa Peachey) were splashing and swimming and having the most wonderful time. McTavish watched them from his position on the boulder. The sun was shining, his coat was still cool and damp, and the boulder was a very nice place for a mid-afternoon nap.

The Peacheys played together in the lake. They had races. They had contests about who could swim the longest distance under water. Ollie became a sea monster and tried to scare Ava. Ava floated on her back and contemplated the ontological enormity of the universe. Betty practised her crawl.

Eventually, they dried themselves off

and plonked themselves down in the sunshine

to get warm. Everyone agreed that it was

the most wonderful feeling to swim in a cold

mountain lake and dry off under the warm sun.

Dozing and chatting, the Peachey family

felt happy and relaxed.

Until Betty looked up.

McTavish was gone!

"McTavish! McTavish! Where are you?"

Betty called his name again and again, but

there was no sign of him.

Betty knew what she had to do. She put

her shoes back on and set off once more, up the mountain, with the rest of the Peachey family scrambling along behind her. They were in far better spirits after their refreshing swim in the mountain lake, filled with energy and optimism, and determined to find McTavish.

"He must be somewhere nearby," said Ava. "McTavish? McTavish!"

"There he is," cried Ollie, spying McTavish far ahead. "What on earth does he think he's doing?"

As the Peacheys came closer, they realised

that McTavish was leaping and playing with a

herd of wild mountain goats.

"Look! There are three baby goats," said

Betty. "I have never seen wild goats before!"

"Nor have I," Ma Peachey said in a hushed voice. "Aren't they beautiful?"

Pa Peachey shook his head. "McTavish is certainly playing with fire now. Those goats

could strike him dead with one sweep of their

deadly horns. They could maim him with a

single kick of their lethal hooves."

"They seem to like him," Ollie said. "Look!

They're playing chase! McTavish is 'it'!"

"How utterly extraordinary," Ava said.

"Two species communing in spontaneous

recreational activity."

"A dog playing with goats!" Betty said,

rather more simply.

Just then, as suddenly as it had begun, the

game ended. McTavish raced off over a small

ridge and disappeared. The goats frolicked

off in the other direction. For a moment, the
Peacheys stood gaping.

Pa Peachey snapped to attention. "Stop
him! Stop him!" he shouted.

"Come back, McTavish!" shouted Ollie and
Ava.

"This absurd dog chase must stop. It is
ruining our day!" Pa Peachey was outraged.

Ma Peachey and Betty exchanged glances.
A strange and knowing look passed between
them, suggesting they shared a secret.

Perhaps they knew what McTavish was
up to. Perhaps they had an idea that he wasn't

really running away. Perhaps they suspected

that, as usual, McTavish had a plan.

Though perhaps he didn't.

You could never really tell with McTavish.

9

Follow that Dog!

The sun was shining. The path up the mountain was shady and cool. It was not very steep, and there were lots of interesting things to look at. But McTavish always seemed to be just ahead of the Peacheys.

Whenever they were certain he had disappeared, one of them glimpsed him peering down from a ledge above. Or saw him vanish into a cave. Or caught sight of him trotting up a path. No matter where they went, McTavish seemed determined to lead them just a little bit further.

Ma Peachey and Betty stopped under a shady tree and sat down.

"Well, we have walked nearly to the top of the mountain," Ma Peachey said. "And a most beautiful walk it has been. It's just a shame we can't catch up with McTavish."

"Yes, that is a shame," Betty said. "It almost seems as if he wants to stay just ahead of us. As if he doesn't really want us to catch up with him. As if he's playing a sort of game with us."

"A 'climb the mountain, swim in the lake and have a lovely walk' sort of game?" Ma Peachey asked.

Betty looked thoughtful. "Yes," she said at last. "Exactly that sort of game."

"It's a shame you didn't bring the picnic lunch," Ollie said. "I'm starving. But there's no point thinking about lunch when it is back in our tent."

Ma Peachey smiled. She reached behind her and held up her rucksack. It looked heavy.

As if it just might, possibly, be full of delicious

things to eat.

"Anyone for lunch?" Ma Peachey asked, and

Betty clapped her hands together with delight.

It was turning out to be a wonderful day.

Ava and Pa Peachey drifted closer at the

sound of the word "lunch". Their sad, forlorn

faces transformed in an instant when they

realised that Ma Peachy had brought the picnic

after all.

A minute later, the entire Peachey family

sat in the shade of a beautiful mountain tree,

eating cheese sandwiches, hard-boiled eggs,

olives, sticks of carrots and celery, with apples

and chocolate for dessert.

"I wonder if McTavish is hungry," said Betty.

"He deserves to be!" said Ollie. "He's led us

on a chase all the way up the mountain, and

now we'll have to walk all the way down again.

What a terrible dog he is."

"McTavish is a rogue and a scoundrel," said

Pa Peachey. "And I have half a mind to return him

to the rescue centre when we find him again."

"UN-rescue him?" Ava said in a shocked

voice.

"Exactly," Pa Peachey said. "Un-rescue

McTavish. He is far too ungrateful to remain rescued. Today has been a nightmare from beginning to end, and who do we have to thank for it? McTavish."

"This lunch isn't a nightmare," said Ollie. "It's amazing."

"The swimming was nice," said Ava, with her mouth full of chocolate.

"The walking was nice," said Ma Peachey, biting into an apple.

"We saw McTavish playing with baby goats," said Betty. "That was something I will never forget."

"Ha. We had to race after that good-for-nothing dog till we were nearly dead of exhaustion. That's something I will never forget," grumbled Pa Peachey.

"Woof," said McTavish.

"Did someone say 'woof'?" asked Pa Peachey.

Ma and Pa Peachey and Ollie and Ava and Betty all turned round at once.

"McTavish!" they all cried together.

For it was he.

"Where have you been?"

"Why did you run away?"

"Good dog, McTavish!"

"Bad dog, McTavish!"

Everyone talked at once. But only Betty said what McTavish really wanted to hear.

"Would you like half of my sandwich?" Betty asked.

"Woof," said McTavish again. In his most polite voice.

So Betty shared her sandwich with McTavish, and he gulped it all down in an instant.

After their lunch, and with McTavish no longer on the run, the Peachey family lazed and chatted for a while in the shade.

"Come on," said Ollie at last. "While we're up here, let's go and see what we can see. Maybe there are some more wild mountain goats or another beautiful place to swim. Let's just go and look."

And then they gathered all the lunch things up and put them back in the rucksack, which Pa Peachey carried this time, and off they went.

That's how it happened that the Peachey family climbed to the very top of the mountain and stood for a long time admiring the view, which went on for a great distance and really

was magnificent.

Then, on their way back down the

mountain, they encountered a deer and her

fawn. They were standing in a beautiful

meadow, and, though the Peachey family were

very close, the deer did not run away for the

longest time.

A bright blue butterfly that none of them

had seen before fluttered just ahead of them on

the path, as if leading them in a new direction.

As they walked, they discovered strange

new birds, a bright green lizard that darted

across the path and more wild flowers than they could count.

They found dozens of shrubs covered in wild blueberries, which they picked and ate by the handful, despite Pa Peachey claiming they were probably poisonous and it would be their last ever meal.

Ava said it would be worth it, as they were so delicious.

The walk down the mountain was more relaxed than the walk up. The Peacheys stopped to swim in the beautiful lake once more. McTavish led the charge into the water, doggy paddling around in circles, swimming from one family member to the next and eventually getting out to sit on the side and dry off in the sun.

McTavish's golden coat spread out on all sides of him as it dried, and when at last he stood up and yawned and stretched into downward dog after a short snooze, he looked just like a teddy Ava had once owned, with a button nose.

Ma Peachey placed one hand on McTavish's fluffy sensible head.

Betty kissed him on his soft furry cheek

and looked deep into his warm brown eyes.

And then, much to her surprise, he winked

at her.

At least she thought he did.

10

Going Home

Nobody wanted to leave Faraway Campsite, but at last they had to fold up the tent and head home.

Ma and Pa Peachey had to get back to work. Ollie had a summer job. And Ava had finished reading all her philosophy books, so it was vital that she get to a library.

In the car, the Peachey family were quiet and companionable. Betty fell asleep leaning on Ollie, and he didn't seem to mind. Ava and Ma Peachey talked about things they might do together later in the summer. Pa Peachey sang campfire songs softly to himself, and sometimes everyone else sang along.

McTavish noted with satisfaction that they seemed like a different family from the one that had set out a few days ago. A better, happier family.

They arrived home at last. Everyone felt tired as they unpacked the car in the dark and piled all the camping equipment in the sitting room.

"Don't worry about it tonight," Ma Peachey said. "We can sort through everything tomorrow."

Pa Peachey and Ava made popcorn for a midnight snack, and the Peacheys all sat together at the kitchen table munching and remembering the best parts of their camping holiday.

While they were talking, McTavish walked over and climbed up into Betty's lap. Betty hugged him tight.

"Sometimes I do wonder," said Betty.

"What do you wonder?" asked Pa Peachey.

"I sometimes wonder if we own McTavish or if he owns us."

"What a silly question," Pa Peachey said. "Of course we own McTavish. We are superior beings, far more intelligent than dogs, with hundreds of thousands more neural connections than any other living creature. Plus, we have opposable thumbs. As the superior being, of course we own the dog and not vice versa. We are humans. McTavish is merely a dog."

Merely a dog? Betty looked at McTavish, who looked back at her with a subtle and complicated expression.

McTavish's expression said a number of things. It said, "I know much more than you could ever imagine." And "Dogs are far cleverer than people give them credit for." His expression also seemed to say, "Sometimes your father talks complete nonsense."

It is possible that Betty interpreted these expressions incorrectly, but it is also possible she did not.

"Well," said Betty. "It may appear that we

own McTavish, but I often have the feeling that McTavish has plans of his own."

"Plans of his own? How absurd," said Pa Peachey.

"Plans of his own? Yes, I think that sounds about right," said Ma Peachey.

Ma Peachey thought about how McTavish managed to get the entire Peachey family up the mountain and into the lake. How he'd managed to organise a lovely picnic at the top of the mountain. How he'd discovered a small flock of wild mountain goats and played with the goats while the delighted Peachey family watched. How he'd led them through meadows

and along paths they never would have seen.

How he'd provided the Peacheys with a perfect

day out in the countryside.

Which was something I couldn't

accomplish, no matter how hard I tried, thought

Ma Peachey.

"You are nothing less than a marvel,

McTavish," said Ma Peachey. "And I am very

glad that you decided to rescue us."

"You're a very good dog, McTavish," said

Betty.

"Woof," said McTavish.

The Countryside Code

"You learn new things and live side by side with nature."

Like Betty says, camping is a wonderful way to experience nature. If you're planning a camping trip or a day out in the countryside, make sure to follow the Countryside Code. This will help you make the most of your trip and protect the environment at the same time.

There are three main things to remember: respect, protect and enjoy!

1. Respect other people

- Think about the people who live nearby, like farmers who are busy working – you don't want to get in the way.

- If you open any gates, close them behind you.

- Be considerate of other people who are enjoying the outdoors. They want to have a nice time, just like you!

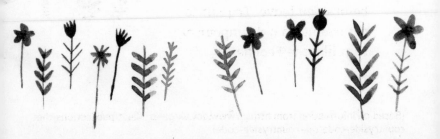

2. Protect the natural environment

- Try not to leave any traces of your visit behind. Litter spoils the beautiful countryside, so be sure to take any rubbish home with you.

- If you have a dog, keep him under control, especially when you're near other animals and other people. McTavish is a very responsible (fictional!) dog, but even a good, obedient dog may chase farm animals if he's not on a lead.

- Don't disturb any plants or wildlife. You should help preserve the countryside so that everyone can continue to enjoy it.

3. Enjoy the outdoors

- Plan ahead before your trip so that you know where to go. You can buy a map or look up the area online.

- Stay safe by following advice or signs on where to go, and by being careful around animals, especially wild ones.

- Check the weather forecast before you leave. Try not to get caught in a downpour of rain like the Peacheys!

(Based on information from https://www.gov.uk/government/publications/the-countryside-code/the-countryside-code)

Packing to go camping

"Pa Peachey dragged a very heavy suitcase into the room. 'I have mosquito repellent for tsetse flies and shark repellent for sharks. I have bottles of aspirin and splints for broken bones. I have bandages and plasters, flares for emergency rescue. I have water purification tablets and whistles. I have face masks in case of hazardous waste, a loudhailer, foil blankets and sterile dressings. I have enough freeze-dried meals for a month in case we are snowed in.'"

Pa Peachey's idea of "the essentials" for camping are a little bit over the top! If you're going camping, here is a checklist of important things you'll need on your adventure:

- [ ] Tent
- [ ] Sleeping bag
- [ ] Air mattress or sleeping mat
- [ ] Torch
- [ ] Map
- [ ] Clothes
- [ ] Towel
- [ ] Soap
- [ ] Toothbrush and toothpaste
- [ ] First aid kid
- [ ] Water
- [ ] Food
- [ ] Plates, bowls and cooking utensils
- [ ] Matches
- [ ] Rubbish bag
- [ ] Sun cream

About ... Meg Rosoff

Meg Rosoff grew up in Boston, America, and moved to London in 1989. Her first novel, *How I Live Now*, has sold over one million copies in 36 countries. Meg has written seven other novels and her books have won or been shortlisted for 23 international book prizes. In 2016, Meg won the Astrid Lindgren Memorial Award – the world's largest children's literature award – the chair of which said of Meg's work, "Each novel is a little masterpiece." Meg lives in London with her family – and their dogs.

"No one writes the way Rosoff does ... I love her fizzy honesty, her pluck, her way of untangling emotion through words" *Daily Telegraph*

"Rosoff's writing is luminously beautiful" *Financial Times*

"A voice so stridently pure and direct and funny that you simply can't question it" *Guardian*

About ... McTAVISH

Meg Rosoff says, "I recently met a dog in my local park with a big head, short legs, wearing a tartan coat and with more attitude than any human I'd ever met. His name was McTavish and he clearly needed a book written about him. The real McTavish hasn't met the excellent people at Barrington Stoke yet, but I feel certain he'd love them."